Hooey Higgins
and the
Tremendous
Trousers

For Lucy Earley
S. V.

For Lorenzo
E. D.

DON'T
MISS:

HOOEY
HIGGINS
AND THE
SHARK

HOOEY HIGGINS
and the
Tremendous
Trousers

STEVE VOAKE
illustrated by Emma Dodson

CANDLEWICK PRESS

Text copyright © 2010 by Steve Voake
Illustrations copyright © 2010 by Emma Dodson

First U.S. edition 2014

Library of Congress Catalog Card Number 2013943994
ISBN 978-0-7636-6923-2

14 15 16 17 18 19 BVG 10 9 8 7 6 5 4 3 2 1

Printed in Berryville, VA, U.S.A.

This book was typeset in Stempel Schneidler and EDodson.
The illustrations were done in ink line and wash.

Candlewick Press
99 Dover Street
Somerville, Massachusetts 02144

visit us at www.candlewick.com

CONTENTS

BANANA
T. P. ROLLS

"HEALTH AND SAFETY, HEALTH
AND SAFETY!" shouted Miss Troutson,
clapping her hands and peering over the top
of her glasses. "What did I say about Health
and Safety?"

Hooey Higgins stopped what he was doing and looked around. The whole class had stopped at the same time, and it was like a freeze-frame from a horror movie: Yasmin Boothroyd had a hammer raised above her head, Ricky Mears was holding a piece of wood with a nail in it in front of his face, and Twig appeared to be trying to saw his legs in half.

Meanwhile, on the far side of the classroom, Robbie Blunt had his hands in the air and Basbo Wilkins was squinting at him over the top of a stapler.

"I want everyone to stop what they're doing and come over to the carpet

IMMEDIATELY.

Hooey was quite pleased in a way. He'd started out with high hopes for his model of a Ferris wheel, but the cheese carton kept falling off the end of the pencil and crushing all the little clay customers. Which, he had to admit, wasn't healthy or safe.

Hooey put down his scissors and stood next to Twig, who had actually been sawing through toilet-paper tubes and was now using one of them as a telescope.

LAND AHOY!

he shouted.

LAND AHOY!

He kept shouting it until Miss Troutson took the tube away.

"All right," she said when everyone was settled. "Can anyone tell me what we covered in our introduction to Building and Engineering last week? Yasmin?"

"STAYING SAFE," said Yasmin.

"Very good, Yasmin. So why do you think I stopped everyone just now?"

"Because people weren't being Healthy or Safe," said Twig. "They were being Unhealthy and Dangerous." He looked at Basbo. "With staplers mainly."

"That is correct," said Miss Troutson as Basbo glared back at Twig. "So your homework this weekend is to come up with a design for something that will make the world a safer place."

"Boring," said Basbo, aiming the stapler at Twig. Twig panicked, jerked his head back, and banged it on the filing cabinet.

"That is *not* the attitude I'm looking for," said Miss Troutson, holding one hand out for the stapler while patting Twig sympathetically with the other. "But I thought a few of you might feel that

way. Which is why I have spoken to the owner
of the fairground and he has agreed to give
a prize to the person who presents the best
safety design in school assembly on Monday."

"Ooh," said Twig, forgetting his injuries.
"Is it cotton candy?"

"Better than that," said Miss Troutson. "The
winner will get free tickets to the fair."

Outside, the day was heavy with heat and sunshine. Little kids monkeyed around by the hedges, Basbo demonstrated wrestling moves on Ricky Mears, and Samantha Curbitt ran circles around the Watson twins before flicking the ball up and scoring her third hat trick.

"She's an angel," said Twig, smiling dreamily. "An angel sent from heaven."
"You shouldn't talk about Basbo like that," said Hooey. "He might hear you."

They watched as Basbo flipped Ricky Mears over his head and dumped him in the shrubbery. "I think he actually wants to kill me," said Twig. "Did you see his face when he aimed the stapler at me?"

"He always looks like that," said Hooey. "Probably just concentrating."

"Yeah, on stapling my head to the wall."

"Never mind that," said Hooey. "Just think about those free tickets. They've got our name on them, Twiggy-boy."

"Maybe we could design something for the hedge-monkeys," said Twig, watching the little kids make their dens in the hedges at the edge of the field. "Something to keep them safe."

"But hedges aren't dangerous, Twig," said Hooey.

"They are if you put the right dog in there," said Twig. "There's one on our street that'll go for anything. He's a complete nutmeg."

"Twig, you're grasping at straws," said Hooey. "Maybe we should just try to get some ideas at the fair tonight."

"OK," said Twig. "I haven't got any money, though. I spent it all on toilet paper."

"*Toilet* paper?"

"Yeah. I needed the rolls for my model of the water chute."

"So what happened to the paper?"

"I wrapped it around some bananas and

put it back.
I thought it
could be like
a surprise treat
for people when
they finish the
roll. You know:

Oooh, a banana!

"That's a bit weird, Twig," said Hooey. "But quite healthy, I suppose. It could help people with their five servings of fruit and veggies a day."

"That could be our design!" said Twig. "BANANA T. P. ROLLS! We could write to the prime minister and everything."

Hooey imagined the look on the prime minister's face when he went to the john and found a banana wrapped in toilet paper. "Maybe we'll come back to that one," he said.

At that moment, Hooey's brother Will arrived, carrying his lunch box in one hand and a notebook in the other. On the front of the notebook he had written: My Decimal Calculations by Will Higgins.

"Ooh, look!" cried Twig, pointing at the cover. "It's Danny the Decimal Point!"

"It's chocolate actually," said Will, scratching it off with his thumbnail. "And who is Danny the Decimal Point?"

"They are in my math group," said Twig. "Danny the Decimal Point and Sammy Subtraction. They live together in Math Mansion with Molly Multiplication and Davina Division."

"I think Will's doing more complicated stuff than that," said Hooey. "Show him, Will."

"OK, listen to this," said Will, flicking through the pages. "I worked out that the average number of cookies eaten by people in this school is 1.97 a day."

Twig pressed his hands to his cheeks with excitement. "One *point* nine seven!" he said. "Wow."

"Wait," said Will. "There's more." He opened his lunch box and produced a cookie from beneath his tuna-fish sandwiches. "I worked out that if you stacked up all the cookies eaten at this school for the next seventy years, the pile would stretch past Mount Everest and all the way into space."

"No *way*!" said Twig. "No wayno wayno *way*!"

Will held up his notebook. "Check it out, Twig. The pictures don't lie."

Hooey peered over Twig's shoulder and saw that Will had drawn a diagram showing lots of kids lying on their backs, with packets of cookies strewn all around them. Another picture showed a snow-topped mountain with a pile of cookies stretching past it into space. Next to it was a huge tower of children, balancing on one another's shoulders. The boy at the top was wearing a helmet and adding more cookies to the pile.

"They just hand 'em up," said Will. "Takes roughly 9.7 hours per cookie."

"Have you got any *actual* photos?" asked Twig hopefully.

"Not yet," said Will. "But it's only a matter of time, Twig. It's only a matter of time."

Hooey cleared his throat. "Umm, Will, leaving the cookies to one side for a moment, can you help us with our project? We need to design something safe."

"Safe?" Will frowned. "What kind of safe?"

"The kind of safe that will win us free tickets to the fair. Miss Troutson's giving them away to the winners of the best safety design. Also, Twig needs some money and we think Basbo wants to kill him."

Twig went slightly pale at the mention of this last bit, but Will just nodded and took a fresh pencil from his pocket.

"What are you thinking, Will?" asked Hooey.

Will licked the end of his pencil and opened his notebook.

"I'm thinking trousers," he said.

A BET WITH BASBO

"Trousers?" said Twig.

"*Interesting,*" said Hooey.

"The way I see it," said Will, "there are three separate tasks." He took his notebook and wrote:

1.   Design something to do with safety.

2.   Get Twig some money.

3.   Keep Basbo from killing Twig.

He turned it around to show Hooey and Twig.

"Yep," said Hooey. "Reckon that about covers it."

Will beckoned Hooey over and whispered in his ear. Hooey listened. Then he smiled.

"What?" said Twig. "What's he saying?"

"Don't worry," said Hooey. "Will's just going to talk to a few people over there. In the meantime, we need to go talk to someone else."

"See you by the hedge," said Will, tucking his pencil in his top pocket.

As Will walked over to Samantha, who was heading a ball for goal number ten, Hooey took Twig by the elbow and walked him across the field.

"I don't get it," said Twig. "Where are we going?"

"To see a friend of yours," said Hooey.

In the middle of the field, Basbo was spinning Johnny Bertram around above his head.

Johnny was yelling, his voice becoming softer as he spun away and louder when he spun back again.

Twig looked at Hooey. "I'm going to die, aren't I?"

"Relax," said Hooey. "No one's going to die. We're just going to have a chat—that's all."

"I can't chat with anyone," said Twig, "if I haven't got a head."

When Basbo saw them, he let go of Johnny Bertram, who sailed off across the grass like a tiny meteorite. He bounced twice, got up and waved, then staggered off toward the monkey bars.

"See?" said Hooey. "Not a scratch on him."

Basbo stared at them for a few moments, then pointed at Twig with a short, stubby finger. "You bunky little bongaweed," he said. "You grizzled me up to Troutson, didn't ya? You opened your flappy-trap and mazzed me up like a minky."

Twig gulped loudly, but Hooey stepped forward and held up his finger. "Um, if I could just interrupt you for a second there, Baz?"

Basbo scrunched up his fists like a couple of cannonballs and scowled so that his eyebrows met in the middle.

"Ya got five seconds, finklewit. I ain't got time for wazzin' with a wozzer like you."

"No, of course you haven't," said Hooey. "But the thing is, I was just having a disagreement with my brother Will over there and I need your help to settle it once and for all."

Basbo frowned. "You want me to fwap him in the bongers?"

"Not really, no," said Hooey hurriedly. "It's just he reckons that Twig here can beat you in a staring contest—"

"What?" said Twig, his voice going up an octave. "When did he—?"

"But *I* said," continued Hooey, "that there's no way Twig could beat you in a million years. I said you could out-stare anyone, anytime, no question about it."

Basbo grabbed Twig by the shirt and pulled him up until their noses were nearly touching. "Think you can beat me, do ya, y'little frambit?"

"No!" squeaked Twig. "I never —"

"Don't worry," said Hooey stepping between them and straightening out Twig's shirt. "When my brother gets these ideas in his head, there's just no stopping him."

He glanced across the field and saw that Will was standing by the hedge with a crowd of people around him. "Why don't you show him, Bazzer? Show him once and for all who's the best starer in Shrimpton-on-Sea!"

Hooey's words seemed to make quite an impression on Basbo. It was as if the leader of the OLYMPIC STARING TEAM had suddenly called to say that their staring champion had unexpectedly been taken ill, and would he, Basbo, mind taking his place? Basbo clenched his fists, his eyes lit up, and he nodded aggressively as if this was the moment he had been waiting for all his life.

"Right, y'little wozzers," he said.

LET'S DO IT!

THE CHAMP

When they reached the other side of the field, Will was standing by the hedge holding a clipboard. A crowd of children and lunch ladies had gathered around him, chattering excitedly.

"Ah, Mr. Bazzer," he said as if he had invited Basbo over for a job interview. "So glad you could come." He turned to Twig. "And you are?"

"I'm Twig," said Twig. "As you already know."

Will nodded and made a note on his clipboard. "Just checking for the record, Twig."

Twig looked bewildered, as if he was having one of those dreams where meerkats ride bicycles and juggle with melons.

Basbo glared at Will. "I hear you reckon this Twiglet's a better starer than me."

Will pushed his glasses back up his nose and nodded. "This is true," he said, "but as a scientist, I am willing to be proven wrong. In fact," he added, "if it turns out that you are better at staring, I will give you twenty pence."

Basbo frowned. "TWENNY PENCE?"

Will took out a silver twenty pence piece and held it up between his finger and thumb. "Twenty pence," he said. "In cash."

Basbo couldn't have looked more surprised if Will had pulled a rabbit from a hat and made it sing the theme from *Star Wars*. "Right," he said. "You're on."

Will turned to Hooey. "If you would like to show the contestants to their seats, then we can begin."

A hush fell over the crowd, and Hooey began to get nervous. Will was usually pretty good at working stuff out, but this was definitely his most ambitious plan yet. If it all went wrong, there was a good chance Basbo would grab all three of them and stuff their heads down the nearest toilet.

"Now then, Bazzer," he said, feeling like the host of a reality show, "if you'd like to come and sit over here, then we can—no, not there, just here, that's it, thank you."

"Are you CRAZY?" hissed Twig in a panicky voice as Basbo sat on the grassy mound opposite him. Basbo was making soft growly noises, like a bad-tempered dog who has heard a rumor that the mailman is coming. All around them, the crowd of children and lunch ladies waited patiently for things to get started. Some of the little kids at the back had even climbed onto the shoulders of the older ones to get a better view.

Hooey patted Twig on the back. "All set, champ?"

"Hooey, I don't know what you're trying to do," said Twig nervously, "but there's no way I'm going to win this. Basbo could stare his way through a brick wall."

"You don't need to win," whispered Hooey. *"That's the beauty of it all."*

As he stepped forward and clapped his hands like a mini Miss Troutson, Hooey realized that he was actually quite enjoying himself. "OK!" he shouted. "IS EVERYONE READY?"

"YAY!" cried the crowd.

TROUSER TROUBLE

Basbo leaned forward and stared until his eyes bulged like soft-boiled eggs.

Twig rested his hands on his knees and raised his eyebrows until they disappeared under his bangs.

"OOOOH!" went the crowd.

"BAS-BO, BAS-BO!" chanted one side.

"TWIG-LET, TWIG-LET!" chanted the other.

Hooey turned to Will. "This is going quite well," he said. "D'you think he could win?"

"Who cares?" said Will. "All that matters is trousers."

"BAS-BO, BAS-BO!"

    "TWIG-LET, TWIG-LET!"

"BAS-BO, BAS-BO!"

    "TWIG-LET, TWIG-LET!"

"BAS-BO!"

    "TWIG-LET!"

"BAS-BO!"

    "TWIG-LET!"

"BAS-BO, BAS-BO!"

    "TWIG-LET, TWIG-LET!"

Basbo stared.

The onlookers

fell silent.

Twig stared.

The onlookers

held their breath.

Basbo stared harder.

Twig stared back

and then . . .

HE BLINKED!

"AWWWWWWW!"
went the crowd.

"YESSSS!" shouted
Basbo, clasping his hands
above his head as everyone
cheered. He walked over to Will
and held out his hand. "Twenny
pence, y'little frarpsichord!"

"Sure thing," said Will, handing
over the money with a flourish. "You
won it fair and square."

"That was great, Basbo," said Hooey.
"But some people might think it was just
a fluke. Maybe you should do it again,
just to prove that you're the absolute total
champion."

"Hooey's right," agreed Will. "And I tell you what: if you do it again, I'll throw in another twenty pence."

Basbo's eyes lit up like two cracked headlights. "Easy money," he growled, sitting on the grass tussock and cracking his knuckles. "Come on, Twiglet, let's see if ya got any more stares in yer stash."

Twig crossed his legs, shut his eyes, and held his hands out in front of him, palms upward. He touched the thumb and forefinger of each hand together and breathed slowly in and out.

"What's up, Twig?" asked Hooey.

"Shh!" said Twig. "I'm meditating."

"Well, do it with your eyes open," said Hooey. "They're all waiting for the second stare-off. Including *Samantha*."

Twig opened one eye and looked at
him. "Samantha? Was that her doing the
TWIGLET-TWIGLET thing?"

"Yup. Her and a couple of lunch ladies.
Now, come on, Twig. Big effort, eh?"

"Right," said Twig, opening his other eye.
"I'm ready."

"**HE'S READY!**" shouted Hooey.

"**HE'S READY!**" cheered the crowd.

"**AND . . . STARE!**" said Hooey.

The crowd went silent.

Basbo stared.

Twig stared back.

Basbo stared some more.

Twig stared back.

Then Basbo began to twitch.

"EH?" went the crowd.

Twig kept staring.

Basbo started to itch and scratch.

"HUH?" went the crowd.

Will winked at Hooey. "And three, two, one . . ." he said.

"YOWCH!" yelled Basbo, jumping up and clutching his trousers. "YOW-OW-OW-OW-OWCH!"

As the crowd gasped, Basbo kicked off his shoes, pulled down his trousers, and ran across the field as if his underpants were on fire, his cries fading as he leaped down the steps and disappeared into the bathrooms.

"YAY!" yelled the crowd. "TROUSERS OFF! TROUSERS OFF! TROUSERS OFF! TROUSERS OFF!"

The lunch ladies began jumping up and down chanting, "TROUSERS OFF! TROUSERS OFF! TROUSERS OFF! TROUSERS OFF!"

Until the chief lunch lady remembered they weren't supposed to shout things like that and made everyone shush up.

As the crowd began to disperse, Hooey turned to see that Twig was sitting with his eyes wide open, still staring at the spot where Basbo had been.

"You can stop now, Twig," said Hooey, waving a hand in front of his face. "Basbo's gone."

Twig looked up at Hooey and blinked. "I had the strangest dream," he said. "People were shouting TROUSERS! and Basbo wasn't wearing any."

"That was no dream, Twig," said Hooey. "That was the real deal."

Twig shook his head. "But why? How? And what about the staring contest?"

"That was just a way of getting Basbo to sit in the same spot for long enough."

Twig looked at Hooey as if he was completely mad. "Why would you want him to do that?"

"Because Will made a bet, that's why."

"I know. He bet Basbo couldn't out-stare me. But he was wrong, wasn't he? So instead of making money, he's lost twenty pence." Twig sighed. "And I thought Will was supposed to be the smart one."

Hooey grinned. "Take a look over there, Twig." He pointed to a corner of the field where Will was standing with his hands cupped in front of him. A large crowd of children and lunch ladies were lining up to give him money.

"What's he doing?" asked Twig.

"Collecting bets."

"But he lost."

"Oh, he lost the staring one. But he also bet he could get Basbo to take his trousers off—and that one is *definitely* paying off."

Twig's eyes widened. "Will bet on that?"

"Yep."

The corners of Twig's mouth began to turn up in the faintest of smiles. "No *way*! No wayno wayno way!"

They turned to look at Will, who appeared to be walking awkwardly, his legs bowing out like a cowboy who has been too long in the saddle. But as he got closer, the reason became clear: his pockets were bulging with coins.

"Shirt, Twig," said Hooey.

Twig pulled up the hem of his shirt, and Will emptied fistfuls of coins into it. As Twig stared open-mouthed at the pouch full of money, Will opened his notebook, took out his pen, and studied his list.

"So let's see here:

Get Twig some money.

Check.

Keep Basbo from killing Twig.

Check.

Design something to do with safety.

Still to do."

Will clicked the top of his pen and put it back in his pocket. "Oh, well. Two out of three's not bad."

"I don't get it," said Twig. "How did you get Basbo to take his trousers off?"

"Easy," said Will. "All we had to do was sit him on an ants' nest."

Twig frowned. He stared at the mound of earth where Basbo had been sitting. He looked at Will. Then, very slowly, he started to smile.

"I think he's got it," said Hooey.

"Right," said Will. "I'm off to the library to

design some insect-proof trousers. I think they could be the next big thing."

"Incredible," said Twig when Will had gone. "How come he's so brainy?"

"Must be all those tuna-fish sandwiches he eats," said Hooey.

"I prefer crackers," said Twig. "Crackers and nuts."

Hooey nodded.

That explains a lot.

BAD NEWS ON THE BUMPER CARS

As Hooey sat with Twig at the top of the
Ferris wheel, swinging the seat and looking
down at the bright lights of the fair, a thought
occurred to him. "You know what would be
amazing?" he said.

"Ooh, hang on, I know this," said Twig.
"Your head exploding. Sticking a toffee apple
up your nose."

"Eee . . . yes," agreed Hooey, studying his
toffee apple at arm's length. "Both those
things *would* be amazing. But actually I was
thinking how great it would be to have insect-
proof trousers."

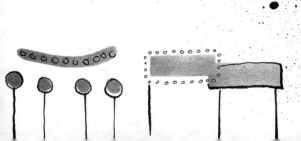

Twig nodded enthusiastically. "Who wouldn't want a pair of those?"

"They wouldn't be just for ants either," Hooey went on. "They could protect you against loads of other stuff too."

"Tremendous!" said Twig.

Hooey stared at him. "That's what we should call them, Twig!" he said. "TREMENDOUS TROUSERS. Or TREMTROWS for short."

"TremTrows," said Twig.

Shweet!

Until now, TremTrows were not something Hooey had ever considered. But as he looked up at the bright lights of the Ferris wheel, he realized that sometimes the simplest ideas are the best.

"The problem is," he said, "we need to work out how to make them before assembly on Monday."

"Problem, shmoblem," said Twig. "My uncle Ernie says that *problem* is just another word for opportunity."

"Is that the same Uncle Ernie who got his leg bitten off by a crocodile?"

"Not all of it. Just a bit off the end."

"And what opportunities did that give him?"

"He got to see the film *Beverly Hills Chihuahua* on the flight home. Which he'd have missed if he'd stayed in Florida."

"Did he enjoy it?"

"Not really. He doesn't like dogs." Twig paused for a moment. "Or crocodiles."

"See, none of that would have happened if he was wearing TremTrows," said Hooey. "The world's crying out for them, Twig. We just need to think hard."

"Thinking gives me a headache," said Twig. "Can't we get Will to do the thinking for us?"

When they got off the Ferris wheel, Will was waiting.

"We've been giving the trouser thing some thought," Hooey told him. "Instead of just insect-proof ones, you could have trousers that protect you against other stuff too. Like crocodiles."

"Or Basbo," said Twig.

"We thought we'd call them TREMTROWS," said Hooey.

Will nodded. "Yep. Makes sense."

Hooey noticed that Will was holding a diagram of himself standing at the hit-a-coconut stall. He had drawn an arrow going from his hand to a coconut and there were lots of numbers written next to it.

"What are those?" asked Hooey.

"They're my calculations," Will explained. He licked his finger and held it up in the air. "Feel that breeze?"

"No."

"Well, there is one. And by my calculations, it's moving at about one kilometer per hour. You know what that means, don't you?"

"We'll stay nice and cool?" suggested Twig.

"No," said Will. "It means it's going to play havoc with my shots. So I'm going to throw the ball slightly to the left, then the wind will blow it back on course and knock the coconut off."

"I didn't know you liked throwing stuff at coconuts," said Twig.

"I don't," said Will. "But if you win, you get to choose a coloring pack with fifty felt pens in it. It's like a rainbow, but with 7.14 times as many colors."

"Seven *point* one four!" said Twig. "Shweet!"

"STEP RIGHT UP, STEP RIGHT UP, STEP RIGHT UP!" shouted the man at the hit-a-coconut stall. "Three balls for a pound."

Will took another look at his drawing, then handed it to Hooey and picked up the first ball. Closing one eye, he drew his arm back, then threw the ball as hard as he could. It thumped into a teddy bear, which slumped forward and fell off the shelf as if it had been shot.

"Hmm, the wind's picked up," said Will. He turned slightly so that his left shoulder was facing forward. This time the ball zoomed off to the right of the middle coconut and thwacked into the straw bales at the back.

"Maybe you should try aiming at the coconuts," said Twig.

"Maybe we should just let Will concentrate," said Hooey.

After stopping to buy some cotton candy and toffee apples, they stood by the bumper cars and watched the cars flying around the track.

"I'm not going on those," said Hooey, shaking his head. "Just look at them. I've never seen such terrible drivers."

Twig peered out from behind his cotton candy. "You're joking, right?"

Hooey grinned. "'Course I'm joking."

As the cars came to a halt, he took a bite from his toffee apple and nudged Twig with his elbow. "C'mon, Twig. Let's go have an accident."

"Ooh, I *love* cotton candy," said Twig, sliding into the passenger seat next to Hooey. "It's like eating a little cloud."

"Yeah, well you might want to try hiding behind it," said Hooey, "'cause Basbo's driving the car over there."

Twig turned pale as he looked at the car on the other side of the circuit. Basbo was crammed into his seat like a troll in a sneaker, and his spiky hair stuck up as if it was trying to suck sparks from the electric grid.

"He's not wearing his seat belt," said Twig. "Maybe I should go and tell him."

"Why?"

"Health and Safety. It's dangerous."

"Not as dangerous as you telling him that it's dangerous. Look at him. He's like a lion watching wildebeests. Just waiting to move in for the kill."

"Thanks, Hooey," said Twig. "That makes me feel a lot better."

"I know something that *will* make you feel better," said Hooey. "I just saw Samantha Curbitt getting into a car over there."

"Yowzee," said Twig, smoothing his hair down. "How do I look?"

"Like a chimp who's found some cotton candy," said Hooey. He put his foot down, turned the wheel, and spun the car out into the center of the track.

"OK, here she comes," said Twig. "Think I'll just act casual."

As they drew alongside each other, he put his elbow on the edge of the car, leaned out, and smiled.

"Hello, Samantha," he said. "You're a good driver."

"Get lost, numpty," said Samantha.

"Can't, I'm afraid," said Twig. "My driver here knows these roads like the back of his hand."

He was trying to think of something else to
say when there was a huge thump. The car
shot sideways, and Twig flew headfirst into
the footwell.

"Take that, y'little weenburgers!" shouted
Basbo.

As Hooey rescued the toffee apple from his
lap, Twig emerged
from the footwell
with his face
covered in cotton
candy.

Hooey grinned.
"I see the airbag
works, then."

"Very funny," said
Twig, scraping lumps of cotton candy
off his face. He was just climbing back into
his seat when there was another thump and
the car spun around in a circle.

"**Way-hey!**" shouted Hooey, clutching his toffee apple and wrestling with the steering wheel. "We're under attack!"

"That was Samantha!" cried Twig excitedly. "Come on, Hooey. Let's get her!"

Hooey pressed his foot down on the accelerator, but as they gathered speed, he noticed that Basbo's car was heading straight for them.

"**Uh-oh,**" whimpered Twig, clamping his hands over his eyes.

"HEALTH AND SAFETY, HEALTH AND SAFETY!"

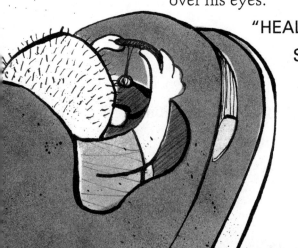

Seconds before impact, Samantha Curbitt's car rammed into the back of Basbo and a fourth car rammed into the back of Hooey. As the cars smashed into one another, the crunch of bumpers was so loud that it sent all the pigeons in the rafters squawking into the air.

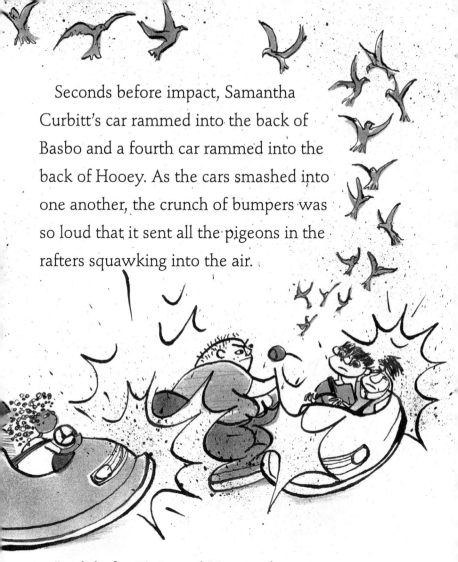

Luckily for Twig and Hooey, they were both wearing their seat belts.

Unluckily for Basbo, he wasn't.

All around the steps of the bumper cars,
people heard the crash and turned to see Basbo
flying out of his seat. Many were surprised
by the fact that such a large boy could soar
through the air with such speed and grace,
even managing to flap his arms a couple
of times along the way. Some said that

if there had been more space, he might
have been the first person ever to fly across
Shrimpton unaided. But unfortunately for
Basbo, space was the one thing he didn't have.

In the ticket booth, Dave the attendant
looked up to see an enormous figure heading
straight for him.

"What the —?" he said, and then a large boy in a football jersey slammed into the window, sending his mug of tea splooshing up the wall over his favorite picture of Kylie Minogue.

Dave watched in horror as the boy slid down the glass with a faint squeaking sound. "OI!" Dave shouted, pointing at a sign that said, PLEASE DO NOT DISTRACT THE OPERATOR. "Can't you read?"

"Come on," said Hooey as Basbo staggered to his feet. "I think we should probably be going."

When they found Will a few minutes later, he was clutching a large pack of felt pens.

"Funniest thing just happened," he said.

"I was throwing my last ball when there was this massive bang and then something came zinging past my left ear. It hit the coconut, which ricocheted off and whacked the man in the you-know-wheres. He was so shocked he just staggered about for a bit and then gave me these."

"Shweet!" said Twig.

"This thing that flew past your ear," said Hooey thoughtfully. "It wasn't red and shiny, was it?"

Will nodded. "I think so. Did you see it too?"

"No," said Hooey with a grin. "But that explains where my toffee apple went."

TREMENDOUS TROUSERS

"The world is a dangerous place," said Hooey as they walked Dingbat along the seafront the next morning. "What with flying toffee apples and all."

"Don't forget flying Basbos," said Twig.

"What we need," said Hooey, "is a pair of trousers that will save us from all these things. And we need them by Monday."

"It's a tall order," said Will. "No doubt about it."

They stopped outside DEREK DANSON'S
DELICIOUS DELICACIES and peered in
through the window. Mr. Danson had built a
model of a Ferris wheel from a construction
kit and as it turned around, little chocolate
truffles swung about in their seats. Above it
was a sign that said:

DEREK DANSON WELCOMES THE
FUNFAIR TO SHRIMPTON-ON-SEA

"That is one classy piece of engineering,"
said Will. "Maybe Mr. Danson will be able to
give us some ideas."

The doorbell dinged as they walked into the shop and Mr. Danson looked up from the counter. "Ah, bonjour, my little chocolatiers," he said. "What can I get for you this morning? Truffles from Transylvania? Caramels from Canada?"

"Just the usual please, Mr. Danson," said Hooey, placing some change on the counter. "Three Crunchies and a bag of toffee bonbons."

"An excellent choice, if I may say so," said Mr. Danson, handing Hooey the Crunchies. "Or perhaps I should say a bon choice, eh? Bonbon!" He chuckled to himself and reached into the jar.

As Mr. Danson was putting the sweets in a bag, Hooey noticed Dingbat sniffing at some empty boxes behind the counter.

"Mr. Danson," he said, "have you finished with those boxes?"

"Indeed I have," said Mr. Danson. "That was my delivery of diet cola. Half the calories means twice the chocolate."

He handed Hooey the toffee bonbons. "You want the boxes?"

"Not really," said Hooey, "but I wouldn't mind the stuff that's in them."

Mr. Danson pulled out a handful of bubble wrap. "This?"

Hooey nodded. "We need to make some special trousers, you see. By Monday."

"Ah, now I understand," said Mr. Danson, tapping the side of his nose. "You are designers, dreamers. Artists like myself, yes?"

"Well, er—"

"Yes, yes! Of course you are! People like us are always on the lookout for the new, the fashionable, the cutting edge! Just as I work magic with *le chocolat*, so you will work your magic with . . . trousers. Am I right?"

"**YES!**" cried Twig, suddenly overcome. "We will make MAGICAL trousers! We will bring **TREMTROWS** to the waiting world!"

Dingbat barked excitedly and began running around in circles. Hooey raised an eyebrow. "Twig," he said, "just help me get the bubble wrap, will you?"

"Sorry," said Twig. "I don't know what came over me."

As they scooped up armfuls of bubble wrap, Hooey noticed Will staring into space. "You OK there, Will?" he asked.

"Shhh!" whispered Mr. Danson, putting a finger to his lips. "I think he is dreaming of your trousers."

"Diet cola . . ." mumbled Will, putting his roll of wallpaper on the counter. "Of course, of *course*."

He unrolled the paper, took a pencil from his pocket, and began scribbling.

"Come on, Will," said Hooey, opening the door. "We need this done before Monday."

"You go ahead," said Will. "I've still got some thinking to do."

"D'you think he's all right?" asked Twig as they walked up the road to Hooey's house.

"He's planning something," said Hooey. "You know what it's like when you suddenly get an idea."

"Nope," said Twig. "Can't say I do."

*   *   *

When they got home, Grandpa was making toast and Grandma was in the living room shouting, "Get down, Vera! Get *down* on that canvas!"

"Is Grandma OK?" asked Hooey.

"She's fine," said Grandpa. "She's boxing on the Nintendo Wii with Mrs. Jenkins."

Hooey peered round the corner to see Grandma and Mrs. Jenkins clutching Nintendo controllers. They were both staring

at the screen and flailing their arms about.

"Hello, dears," called Grandma as Dingbat barked and thumped his tail on the floor. "I'm just opening up a can of SMACKY-PUNCH on Vera."

"OH, YEAH?" shouted Vera. "Well take that! And that! And *that*!"

"I'll say one thing for your gran," said Twig as they sat at the kitchen table. "She's got a mean left hook."

"You should see her on Pro Wrestling," said Grandpa. "No one can get near her."

"Grandpa," said Hooey, "I don't suppose you've got any spare trousers?"

Grandpa patted his pockets. "Fresh out, I'm afraid. But I can check upstairs if you like. What d'you need them for?"

"We need to make some special ones," said Hooey. "For Emergency Purposes."

"I see," said Grandpa. He took a bite of toast, then fed the rest to Dingbat. "What kind of emergencies did you have in mind?"

"Oh, you know," said Twig, "fairground accidents, flying toffee apples, that kind of thing."

Grandpa nodded. "Well you can never be too careful. Although I think my trousers might be a bit on the roomy side."

"They're not for me," said Hooey. "They're for Twig."

"**Eh?**" said Twig. "Why me?"

"Because they're going to need very special testing," said Hooey. "And *you* are a Very Special Tester."

Twig smiled. "I'm a Special Tester," he said.

"What we need is *expandable* trousers," said Hooey. "Big, stretchy, expandable ones."

Grandpa thought for a moment. "I know the very thing," he said, and disappeared out the back.

"Big stretchy expandable ones?" said Twig. "What for?"

"Three reasons," said Hooey. "One: You need to feel comfortable. Two: You need to look normal. And three: We need to stuff a load of bubble wrap down your trousers."

"How's having bubble wrap down my trousers going to make me look normal?" asked Twig.

"I'm not going to lie to you, Twig," said Hooey. "It's going to be tricky. But I'm confident we can do it."

"We?" said Twig. "You're not the one who has to wear them."

"How about these?" asked Grandpa as he walked back into the kitchen. "Grandma doesn't wear them much now that she's got the Nintendo."

Hooey and Twig stared at the huge pair of bright-yellow sweatpants that Grandpa was holding up.

"Perfect," said Hooey.

Twig looked at Hooey and then back at the sweatpants again.

"You have *got* to be kidding."

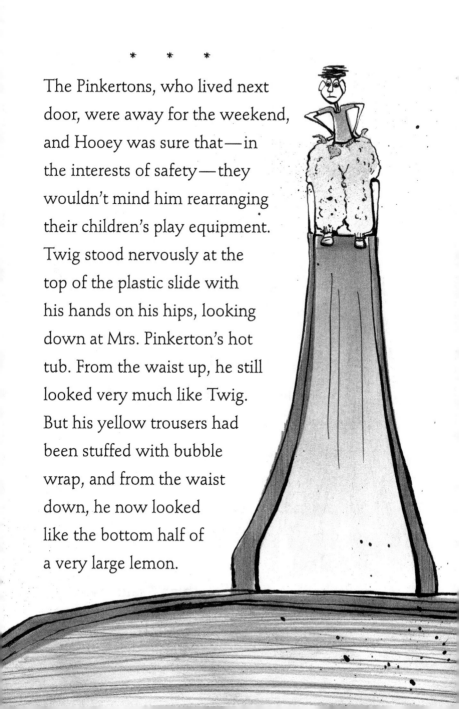

The Pinkertons, who lived next door, were away for the weekend, and Hooey was sure that—in the interests of safety—they wouldn't mind him rearranging their children's play equipment. Twig stood nervously at the top of the plastic slide with his hands on his hips, looking down at Mrs. Pinkerton's hot tub. From the waist up, he still looked very much like Twig. But his yellow trousers had been stuffed with bubble wrap, and from the waist down, he now looked like the bottom half of a very large lemon.

"OK," said Hooey. "By re-creating an unfortunate fairground incident, we'll be able to see how much protection the trousers offer." He looked at the slide and the hot tub. "It's supposed to be a log ride, like at the fair. Obviously you'll need to use your imagination a bit."

"I am using my imagination," said Twig. "I'm imagining myself in an ambulance on the way to hospital."

"Positive thinking, Twig," said Hooey. "That's what we need."

"Do people fall out of log rides a lot?" asked Twig.

"Safety's all about preparation," said Hooey, "and if somebody *did* fall out of a log ride, you can bet the first thing they'd say would be: Thank goodness for my TremTrows."

"Probably not the first thing," said Twig.

"They'd probably go ARGGGHH! first."

"Well, whatever. But at some point, I'm sure they'd be grateful." Hooey opened his camera phone and got Twig in the center of the picture. "Smile, Twig. You're the new Face of TremTrows."

Twig smiled and waved. "Shweet."

"OK, down to business," said Hooey when he'd taken the picture. "Skateboard?"

Twig unhooked the skateboard from the rungs of the ladder and held it up. "Check."

Hooey threw him the flowery pink cushion he had borrowed from Grandma. "Crash helmet?"

"Check," said Twig, securing it to his head with an elastic band. "TremTrows fully bubble-wrapped?"

Twig punched himself in the leg and nodded. "Check."

78

"OK, Twig, let's run through it one more time. You're on a log ride at the fair, possibly with your family."

"Oooh, this is so enjoyable and lovely!" cried Twig happily.

"Good. That's the idea," said Hooey.

"When we've finished, I'm going to buy you all an ice cream!"

"OK, Twig, that's very convincing, but now you need to focus because we're going to do the test."

"What test?"

"You know. Something goes wrong and you fall *out* of the log ride."

"Oh, no!" said Twig. "What about my family?"

"There *is* no family."

"But I promised to buy them an ice cream."

"Twig, they're not real, remember? We're just *imagining* this."

"Oh, right. Sorry."

Twig sat on the skateboard and clutched the handrail at the top of the slide. "Oh, no, everyone," he said to his imaginary family. "There's a problem with the log ride. I think there's been some kind of malfunction. . . ."

"Wait for it," said Hooey, holding up his phone. "I'll say three, two, one, *action*—and on *action,* just push yourself down the slide and act terrified in a log-ride emergency kind of way. Then I'll do a close-up on your trousers to demonstrate how they save your life."

"OK," said Twig. "Gotcha."

Hooey pointed his phone at Twig and lined him up on the screen. "OK. THREE . . ."

Twig tensed his muscles.

"TWO . . ."

Twig gritted his teeth.

"ONE . . ."

Twig shut his eyes.

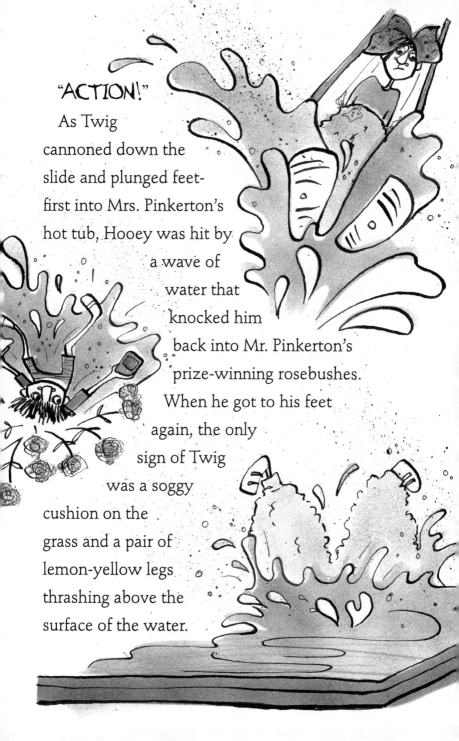

"ACTION!"

As Twig cannoned down the slide and plunged feet-first into Mrs. Pinkerton's hot tub, Hooey was hit by a wave of water that knocked him back into Mr. Pinkerton's prize-winning rosebushes. When he got to his feet again, the only sign of Twig was a soggy cushion on the grass and a pair of lemon-yellow legs thrashing above the surface of the water.

"That's good," called Hooey, zooming in on them with his camera. "Now come up so I can get a shot of your face."

There was silence for a moment and then Twig rose out of the water with a strangled cry before flapping over the side like a demented flounder. "TremTrows malfunction," he gasped.

ABORT! ABORT!

"That was excellent," said Hooey as Twig blew out a mouthful of water and rolled over onto his back. "Great acting, Twig!"

"I wasn't acting," said Twig. "Those trousers nearly killed me!"

"Shush, shush, shush!" said Hooey, hurriedly turning off his camera phone. "You have to stress the safety aspect. That's the whole point."

"Well, I'm sorry," replied Twig, "but the whole point is that they tried to drown me. My head went down and my legs went up. If these trousers had had their way, I'd still be down there now."

Hooey looked at Twig sitting in a puddle, bits of bubble wrap protruding from his trousers. "Maybe we should try it without the water," he said. "Just have you falling in some rosebushes or something."

"No way," said Twig, pulling off the trousers. "I've had enough pain for one day."

"But you're the Special Tester," said Hooey.

"Not any more," said Twig. "I quit."

"Hang on, Twig," said a voice. "Don't quit yet."

Hooey and Twig turned to see Will standing at the gate with a two-liter bottle of cola in each hand. He put down the bottles, pulled a roll of wallpaper from his blazer pocket, and smiled.

"Just wait," he said, "until you see my plan."

TIGHTS AND TOILETS

"Now then, now then!" shouted Miss
Troutson, clapping her hands. "Our very
special Health and Safety assembly is only ten
minutes away, and we don't want to keep the
rest of the school waiting. So make sure your
presentations are ready, and don't forget to
bring everything with you."

"Um, Miss Troutson," said Hooey when the other children had scurried away to their desks. "Can I go and help Twig get ready?"

Miss Troutson peered at him over the top of her glasses. "Whatever do you mean, child?"

"He's in the boys' room undergoing some technical adjustments."

"Technical adjustments?"

"Yes. Will's doing it."

"Ah, yes, *your brother,*" said Miss Troutson, seeming to relax when she heard Will's name. "A sensible, hard-working boy. Well, run along, then. But make sure you're in the gym by quarter past ten."

"Yes, Miss Troutson," said Hooey.

His fingers tingled with excitement as he thought about Will's latest plan. It was a brilliant idea, no doubt about it, and as he walked along the corridor, he imagined himself standing in front of the whole school as they clapped and cheered and threw flowers at his feet. *"It was really nothing,"* he would say, catching a bouquet and bowing modestly. *"I couldn't have done it without my brother Will or my brave friend Twig."*

He imagined being carried out of the assembly on people's shoulders, everyone shouting, *"Three cheers for Hooey! Three cheers for—"*

"HOOEY, where have you been?" said Will, sticking his head around the door of the boys' room. "We've been waiting ages."

"Sorry," said Hooey, his dream dissolving in a whiff of disinfectant. "Had to get permission from the Big Fish."

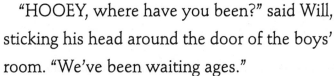

He followed Will into the boys' room and saw that Twig was standing by the stalls wearing nothing but a T-shirt and a pair of tights.

Hooey grinned. "You look nice."

"Don't, Hooey. I mean it," said Twig. He made a little space between his finger and thumb. "I am *this* far from quitting."

"OK, sorry," said Hooey, holding up his hands. He turned to Will. "Where are the TremTrows?"

"In there," replied Will, gesturing toward one of the stalls. "Hanging up next to the dress."

"The *dress*?" said Twig, a look of horror on his face. "No one said anything about a dress!"

"Don't worry," said Hooey. "It's just to hide the TremTrows until the last moment. We borrowed a wig from Mrs. Jenkins, and we're going to introduce you as Mrs. Twiggleton."

"Right, that's it," said Twig, peeling off his tights. "I'm out of here."

"Wait," said Hooey. "If you do this, you could go down as the first person to wear TremTrows in the whole of history. Ever."

"I don't care."

"Samantha will, though."

Twig stopped, tights wrinkled around his knees. "What?"

"I told Samantha you were going to surprise everyone in assembly, and she said, 'Wow. Twig's so *cool.*'"

Twig's eyes widened. "Samantha said that?"

"Sure did. Think about it, Twig. In ten minutes' time, you could be the coolest kid in school."

Twig smiled. "Well, if you put it like that . . ."

He bent over and began tugging up his tights again.

Will sighed and picked up the two bottles of cola. "Hooey, help me shove these down his tights, will you?"

Twig pulled his tights open, and Hooey pushed one bottle down his left leg with the neck pointing upward.

"Steady," said Twig nervously as Will shoved the other one down his right leg. "I don't want to explode."

"Relax," said Hooey, twisting the cap of the bottle until it hissed. "These bad boys will only go off on your say-so."

The bathroom door squeaked open, and a small blond kid stood in the doorway, holding a plastic cup and hiccuping softly. His eyes widened as he stared at the scene before him.

"What's up?" said Twig. "Haven't you ever seen a girl with soda down her tights before?"

The small boy shook his head and hiccuped some more.

"Well, that's why you come to school," said Will as Hooey filled the boy's cup with water and gave it back to him. "It's called an education."

"There's a lesson he won't forget in a hurry," said Hooey as the sound of tiny hiccups faded up the corridor. "Dress to Impress, by Mrs. Twiggleton."

"Look, can we just get on with this before he brings his whole class back for a guided tour?" said Twig irritably.

"OK, fine," said Will. "Balloons?"

"Balloons," said Hooey, producing two from his pocket. They were the long thin ones with knobbly bits up the sides.

"Perfect," said Will. "Mints?"

"You've got them, remember?"

"Oh, yeah." Will rummaged around in his bag for a few seconds before pulling out two packets of chewy mints.

"Mints?" said Twig, frowning. "What are they for?"

"Not just *any* old mints," said Hooey as Will held them out like magic wands. "These are the secret ingredient of our all-new Super TremTrows."

"Really?" said Twig. "*Super* TremTrows?"

"Yeah, but you need to be careful," said Will, opening the mints and pushing them into one of the balloons. "These things are super-powerful."

"What you have to do," said Hooey, dropping mints into the other balloon, "is make sure you only drop in *one mint at a time*."

"I don't understand," said Twig. "Drop it where?"

"In here," said Hooey, unscrewing the cola bottle cap and pushing the neck of the balloon over the end.

"Here's how it works," said Will. He unrolled a piece of wallpaper and taped it to the mirror. "This is you," he said, using his ruler to point to a smiling stick figure with big ears. "And these are the bottles in your tights."

"With you so far," said Twig.

"Now, the balloons—*here*—are full of mints, right?"

"Right."

"So it's important that you keep your hands in your pockets and squeeze the balloons until you're ready to activate the trousers."

"Why?"

"Because when you let go, the mints will fall into the cola and make a gas that will blow the balloons up in a safe and healthy way, thus protecting you from the world and all its dangers."

"The only slight, teensy-*weensy* problem," said Hooey, "is that we haven't had a chance to test it yet."

Twig chewed the side of his thumb nervously. "Is that bad?"

"Not *bad*, exactly. It's just that Will only had enough money for two bottles of cola, so we don't know exactly how many chewy mints to use. But as long as you only drop in one at a time, you'll be fine. Won't he, Will?"

"Absolutely," said Will, slipping elastic bands over the neck of the balloons. "Just remember to take these off before you go in and hold on to the mints until you're ready. OK?"

"OK," said Twig.

Hooey heard the chatter of children making their way toward the gym and allowed himself to think about the moment when the free tickets to the fair would finally be theirs.

"Twig," he said, sliding his mum's makeup bag along the floor, "put your dress on and make yourself pretty. We've got a competition to win!"

TWIG TAKES OFF

"GOOD MORNING, EVERYONE," said Mr. Croft, the principal.

"GOOD MORNING, MR. CROFT!" chorused two hundred and twenty-three children.

Meanwhile, the two hundred and twenty-fourth looked at himself in the mirror and saw a strange woman called Mrs. Twiggleton staring back at him. "What to choose, what to choose?" he said, reaching for the eye shadow. "*Flutter Me Beautiful* or *Hello, Pussycat?*"

Back in the hall, Hooey sat cross-legged on the end of the row, waiting for the presentations to begin.

"Now, then," continued Mr. Croft, "Miss Troutson's class has been working on a project called **STAYING HEALTHY, STAYING SAFE**. So this morning we have a very special assembly in which the children will share some of the things they have been doing."

Miss Troutson nodded encouragingly, and Hooey led the line of children to the front of the gym, where they stood clutching bits of paper, paintings, and junk models. As Ricky Mears stepped forward, the front row of kindergarteners wiggled and squirmed and waved at him.

Ricky was about to wave back when the kindergarten teacher put on her stern face and went *shush, shush, shush!* while Miss Troutson glared at Ricky and hissed, *"Get on with it!"*

Ricky cleared his throat, held up his piece of paper, and said in a loud voice, "We have been learning how to be Healthy. We have been learning how to be Safe. This is the things what we have been learning."

As Miss Troutson smiled and mouthed *Well done* at him, Basbo stepped forward and held up several pieces of wood that had been roughly nailed together in the shape of a club.

"The world's a dangerous place, innit?" he said. "If you get attacked by tigers or dinosaurs, you're gonna need to get yourself one of these."

"YAY!" shouted the little kids.

Bazzer waved his club at them and made caveman noises:

UG-UG-UG-UG-EURGGGH!

The little kids shrieked happily, clutching their heads and falling backward into the row behind.

"No, no, *NO!*" shouted Miss Troutson, striding up to the front and snatching Basbo's club away. She turned to the principal and smiled thinly. "Sorry about that," she said. "I think Barry must have got a little bit confused."

She put the club behind the piano and nudged Basbo with her elbow. "Show them your poster," she hissed.

Sulkily, Basbo held up a poster that said:

STAY SAFE
DON'T GO OUT

"Hmmm," said the principal. "Interesting."

"It was all a bit last-minute," explained Miss Troutson apologetically. "But I actually think Barry has worked extremely hard on his drawing."

Basbo's picture showed someone peering out through a window. They were dressed in what appeared to be a suit of armor with wire coming out of it. The end of the wire was plugged into a socket.

"It's electric," said Basbo. "Anyone touches you and KER-BAM! End of story."

"Right, thank you, Barry," said Miss Troutson hurriedly. She turned to Sarah-Jane Silverton. "Sarah-Jane, perhaps you'd like to tell everyone about *your* idea?"

"Certainly, Miss Troutson," said Sarah-Jane.
"It would be my pleasure."

She reached down
and picked up a
shoe box, which
she had painted
red and gold.
As the morning
sunlight streamed
through the gym
windows, the shoe
box sparkled and
shone like a gift from
heaven.

"Ooooh!" went the little kids.

Uh-oh, thought Hooey. *Serious competition.*

"This may look like an ordinary shoe box,"
said Sarah-Jane in her tinkly, musical voice,
"but inside is a special lesson for us all on how
to be healthy *and* safe."

She released a tiny silver catch on the edge of the box and the side dropped down to reveal a miniature doll's house. Everyone in the hall gasped as Sarah-Jane held it up to show the tiny furniture hidden inside. A little family of dolls was seated at the table, enjoying a small but healthy supper.

Hooey looked over and saw that Mr. Croft actually had tears in his eyes. His hands were clasped to his chest, and he appeared to be whispering the words *so* and *beautiful* over and over again.

Will was looking worried. As Sarah-Jane said, "I would now like to take you on a short tour of Dolly's World, pointing out matters of Health and Safety along the way . . ."

Hooey sidled over to Miss Troutson and whispered, *"Miss, I need to get Twig. He's still in the boys' room."*

"What?" Miss Troutson frowned. "Why?"

"He's getting ready."

"Oh, run along, then," said Miss Troutson, anxious not to miss any more of Sarah-Jane's presentation. "But hurry up. You're on next."

When Hooey got to the boys' room, Twig was still putting on his makeup.

"I wasn't sure which lipstick to go for," he said. "In the end I went for *Kiss Me Pink*." He smacked his lips against a paper towel and looked in the mirror. "What d'you think? Too much?"

"Never mind all that," said Hooey. "Grab your mints and release the bands. We're on next."

*   *   *

Back in the gym, Sarah-Jane was coming to the end of her presentation. "And that's why," she was saying, "it's important to be Healthy *and* Safe . . ." Picking up the tiniest doll, she paused for effect, smiled at the kids and added, "How*ever* small you are!"

"BRAVO!" shouted Mr. Croft as the staff rose from their seats to applaud. "BRAVO!"

"OK," said Hooey as they waited outside the gym doors. "Things aren't looking great. But if you play it cool and don't inflate your trousers too early, we still have a chance."

As Sarah-Jane went back to her place, Hooey walked to the front of the gym and stood with his hands on his hips, waiting for silence.

"Keeping dolls healthy and safe is one thing," he said when everyone had quieted down. "But what happens if you're not a doll? What then? *Hmm?*"

All around the room, teachers turned to one another and nodded, recognizing that Hooey had asked an important question.

"I'll tell you what, then," Hooey continued. "That's the time to get yourself some EXTRA-SPECIAL PROTECTION. Ladies and gentlemen, please put your hands together for . . .

MRS. TWIGGLETON!"

The door swung open, and Twig appeared, his lilac dress swishing as he flounced down the aisle.

Miss Troutson peered over the top of her glasses as if she couldn't quite believe what she was seeing. Everyone else pointed and chattered excitedly until Hooey held up his hands for quiet.

"OK," said Hooey. "Mrs. Twiggleton will now demonstrate an amazing new invention that could save your life. Isn't that right, Mrs. Twiggleton?"

"That's right, dear," said Twig in a high, squeaky voice. "Safety first."

"Bless her," said Hooey. "She's *so* brave. Samantha, if you wouldn't mind?"

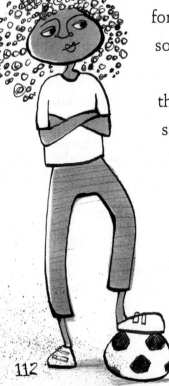

Samantha Curbitt stepped forward and placed a soccer ball on the floor.

"Now, we all know that soccer can be fun," said Hooey. "But imagine if Mrs. Twiggleton was standing behind the goal and someone missed a penalty shot. What would happen *then*?"

Will immediately put his hand up and Hooey pointed to him. "Yes, Will?"

"I imagine, Hooey, that she would be in a great deal of DANGER."

"He's right, ladies and gentlemen," said Hooey. "At least, *normally* she would. But underneath this dress, Mrs. Twiggleton is wearing something that will offer her maximum protection. Underneath this dress, Mrs. Twiggleton is wearing a pair of SUPER TREMTROWS!"

Hooey was about to signal
for Twig to release a couple
of the mints when he saw
Samantha walk backward and start to take a
run-up.

He just had time to shout, "NOT YET,
SAMA —" before she blammed the ball as
hard as she could
into Twig's lower
portions. Twig
flew backward
and crashed into
the music cart,
sending chime bars
flying in all directions.

"Oh, good grief!" cried the principal.
"Are you all right, Mrs. Twiggleton?"

Twig staggered to his feet and gave a
lopsided smile. "I'm fine!" he squeaked. "And it's all
thanks to my TremTrows!"

There was a loud cheer and, just for a few seconds, Hooey thought they might actually have a chance of winning. But as Twig put his thumbs up, Hooey heard the faint rattle of mints, followed by a plopping sound. There was a loud fizzing, and then Twig's dress slowly began to swell up like some strange, bloated jellyfish.

"**Uh-oh,**" said Twig.

The little kids gasped.

Miss Troutson crossed herself.

Then, as the huge, cola-filled balloons began lifting the bottom of Twig's skirt, Mr. Croft started to run for the doors, shouting, **"TAKE COVER, EVERYONE! I THINK MRS. TWIGGLETON'S GONNA BLOW!"**

But he was too late.

With a noise that could be heard in the village center, three miles away, Twig's trousers exploded, drenching the whole room with a soggy mixture of diet cola and chewy mints.

Mr. Bilks, the janitor, watched in horror as the gym's walls suddenly turned brown, as if a vat of gravy had exploded inside a microwave.

Hooey opened his eyes to see the front four rows of children sitting in stunned silence, their hair blown backward by the force of the blast. Miss Troutson sat in her chair

with her mouth open, diet cola dripping from the end of her nose. And at the back of the hall, Mr. Croft stood with one hand still reaching for the door, the outline of his body imprinted on the wall behind him.

At that moment, Twig appeared in the doorway to the PE closet with his clothes in shreds. "Has anyone seen my trousers?" he asked. Then he fell back into the closet again.

"**HOOEY HIGGINS,**" said Miss Troutson, standing up and folding her arms as a sticky pool of cola began to form around her shoes. "Was this *your* idea, by any chance?"

Hooey nodded. "Yes, it was. But I've got some better ones."

He smiled hopefully.

"Do you want to hear them?"

SANDERSON'S SURPRISE

"Never mind, love," said Hooey's mum as the family sat down for dinner. "You did your best, which is all that matters."

Hooey shook his head. "That's not what Miss Troutson said. She said what matters is not blowing your trousers up in assembly."

Will nodded. "She was actually very clear on that point."

"So what went wrong, then?" asked Dad, helping himself to some potatoes.

"Twig used too many mints," said Will. "I told him not to, but he just went ahead and tossed the whole lot in."

"To be fair," said Hooey, "I think he lost concentration when Samantha's soccer ball whacked him in the you-know-wheres."

"That's why I always lose to your grandma at tennis on the Wii," said Grandpa.

"It's your own fault," said Grandma. "You stand too close when I'm serving."

There was a loud knock at the door, and Grandpa pushed his chair back. "I'll get it," he said, winking at Hooey. "I don't want to stand too close to Grandma while she's serving."

Hooey rested his chin on the palm of his hand and watched Grandma dish up the vegetables. He'd been so sure that the TremTrows would win the competition. He'd imagined celebrating at the fair with Twig and Will, going on all the free rides and having a crazy time.

But instead the prize had gone to Sarah-Jane Silverton and her Dollies from Dullsville. Hooey guessed she'd probably just take them for a quick ride on the teacups and go straight home again.

He sighed.

All that work.

All that work for nothing. . . .

"Hooey," called Grandpa. "There's someone at the door to see you."

"Me?"

"Yes, it's a Mr. Sanderson. Says he wants to talk to you about his son."

Pushing his plate to one side, Hooey walked out into the hallway and was alarmed to find a very large man standing at the door with his arms folded. He wore big clumpy boots, and his arms were covered with tattoos of anchors and swords with fierce-looking snakes wrapped around them.

"Um, hello," said Hooey nervously. "Can I help you?"

"That depends," said the man gruffly. "Are you Hooey Higgins?"

Hooey nodded.

"And are you the person responsible for the exploding trousers?"

"Which ones?" asked Hooey, hoping the man had got him mixed up with some other exploding-trouser incident.

"The ones at school."

Hooey's face fell. "I'm afraid so," he said.

The man leaned on the doorframe. "You do realize," he said, "that you scared the living daylights out of my son Sammy today?"

"I'm sorry," said Hooey, trying to remember if he knew anyone named Sammy Sanderson. "But I don't think . . ."

"He said there were three of you," said the man. "Is that right?"

Since he already seemed to know all the details, Hooey guessed there was no point in denying it. "Yes," he said. "But I can't give you their names."

"Twig and Will, wasn't it?"

"Yep, that's them."

Hooey was just wondering if he could make a run for it when he looked up and saw, to his surprise, that the man had a huge smile on his face.

"Well, I just came round to say thanks," he said.

"Huh?" said Hooey.

"You have no idea what it's been like these past few weeks," the man continued. "Morning, noon, and night, on and on and on, driving the whole family nuts."

"Huh?" said Hooey again.

"My son Sammy. Three weeks we've had to put up with his blinkin' hiccups. Three weeks! But then you come along, blow your trousers up, and that's it, job done. Cured him in an instant!"

It was then that Hooey remembered the little blond boy in the bathroom. "So you're not mad, then?"

"Mad?" replied the man. "I'm over the moon, my son! And just to prove it, I've brought you something to say thanks."

He pulled an envelope from his back pocket

and handed it to Hooey. "It's not much, but it's the least I can do. Anyway, thanks again, mate."

Hooey watched him go and then walked back into the dining room with the envelope in his hand.

"Who was that?" asked Will. "He looked a bit scary."

"He was nice actually," said Hooey. "Just came to say thanks for blowing up Grandma's trousers."

"I must be getting old," said Grandma, peering down at her nylon slacks. "I didn't even notice."

"You know who he is, don't you?" said Dad.

"Sammy Sanderson's dad apparently," said Hooey.

"Well, yes. But he also happens to own the fairground." Dad smiled and picked up a serving dish. "More peas, anyone?"

Hooey stared at the envelope in his hand.

"Will," he said, "get me the phone."

Twig was in his bedroom when the phone rang.

"Hello?" he said. "Twig's residence."

As he listened to what Hooey had to say, Twig stared out the window and watched the colored lights of the fair flickering on in the distance.

"Go on, then," he said nervously. "Open it."

Back at Hooey's house, everyone fell silent as Hooey tore open the envelope.

"Well?" whispered Twig. "Is it what you thought it was?"

Hooey peered inside the envelope and grinned.

"You'd better believe it, Twiggy-boy," he said, pulling out the contents and waving them in the air. "We've done it! WE'VE GOT THREE FREE TICKETS TO THE FAIR!"

Then as Will jumped out of his chair and Dingbat began barking excitedly, Hooey took the phone from his ear and held it up so that everyone could hear the sound of Twig dancing around his bedroom, cheering and yelling and shouting at the top of his lungs . . .

SHWEET!

SHWEET!